TINY TIGER'S SQUEAKY SWEATER

By
Moira Neal

Illustrated by
Nell Game

BARRON'S

Woodbury, New York • Toronto • Sydney

Many thanks to Nell for her beautiful illustrations, and to Tony; without his help this book wouldn't have been possible!

First U.S. edition published 1986 by Barron's Educational Series, Inc.
Barron's Educational Series, Inc. has exclusive publication rights in the U.S.A., Canada, Australia, and South Africa.

All inquiries should be addressed to:
Barron's Educational Series, Inc.
113 Crossways Park Drive
Woodbury, New York 11797

International Standard Book No. 0-8120-5767-8
Library of Congress Catalog No. 86-14121

Library of Congress Cataloging-in-Publication Data

Neal, Moira.
 Tiny Tiger's squeaky sweater.

 Summary: Tiny Tiger wins a visit to the Land of Squeaks, where the friendly bears give him a sweater with magic powers. Pressing the pictures produces a squeaking noise.
 1. Toy and movable books—Specimens. [1. Tigers—Fiction.
2. Bears—Fiction. 3. Magic—Fiction. 4. Toy and movable books]
I. Game, Nell, ill. II. Title.
PZ7.N2544Tk 1986´ [E] 86-14121
ISBN 0-8120-5767-8

Printed in Singapore by Tien Wah Press

For Claire and Gareth...

and you!

Tiny Tiger was sitting at his breakfast table one morning eating his bowl of cereal. Suddenly he noticed a contest on the back of the cereal box.

"Win a holiday to the Land of Squeaks," it said.

Tiny thought it sounded like fun, and so he decided to enter.

MATCH THE FOOTPRINTS
and win a holiday....

Name _____

EEEK!

EEEK!

All he had to do was match six footprints with the right creatures.

They belonged to a dog, a cat, a bird, a rabbit, a duck, and a mouse.

Can you help him decide which is which?

When he had finished he popped his entry into an envelope and went outside to get his tricycle.

He was in a hurry to mail his letter as quickly as he could. He didn't notice Mrs. Mouse, who was out for a walk.

"Squeak!" she cried as he ran over her tail. Why is Tiny in such a hurry? she wondered.

Soon he arrived at the post office, which was owned by Mrs. Mirabelle Mouse.

He paid five hazelnuts for the stamp and mailed his letter into the hole in the tree.

A few days later Mr. Percival the Postman brought him a long white envelope with his name on it. "Who can this be from?" he whispered. He opened it quickly and read it out loud. It said:

Dear Tiny Tiger,

I am very happy to say that you have won first prize in our contest. Well done! Your holiday in the Land of Squeaks will start next Monday, and we will pick you up at nine o'clock in the morning.

Furry Bear

Tiny was so excited that he jumped up and down so hard that he hit his head on the ceiling.

He went to the cupboard under the stairs to find his suitcase. "Squeak!" it went as he opened the door. Hmmmm ….I must oil that door some time, he thought to himself.

The next day he packed his case with all the things he would need. He had to sit on it because it was so full.

On Sunday night Tiny was so excited that he couldn't sleep at all. He got up early and had his breakfast.

At exactly nine o'clock he heard a very loud squeaking sound coming from outside. He looked out of the window to see what it was.

Standing in front of his house was a very large, shiny red helicopter.

On the side of it were the words "Bearairways—Land of Squeaks."

The pilot, a very large brown bear, jumped out and greeted Tiny Tiger. "Congratulations!" he said. "If you would like to collect your baggage we'll be off."

Tiny struggled with his case, but soon they were safely on board the helicopter. The mouse family all "squeaked" goodbye to him and wished him well.

He waved to all his other friends and climbed into the helicopter next to the pilot.

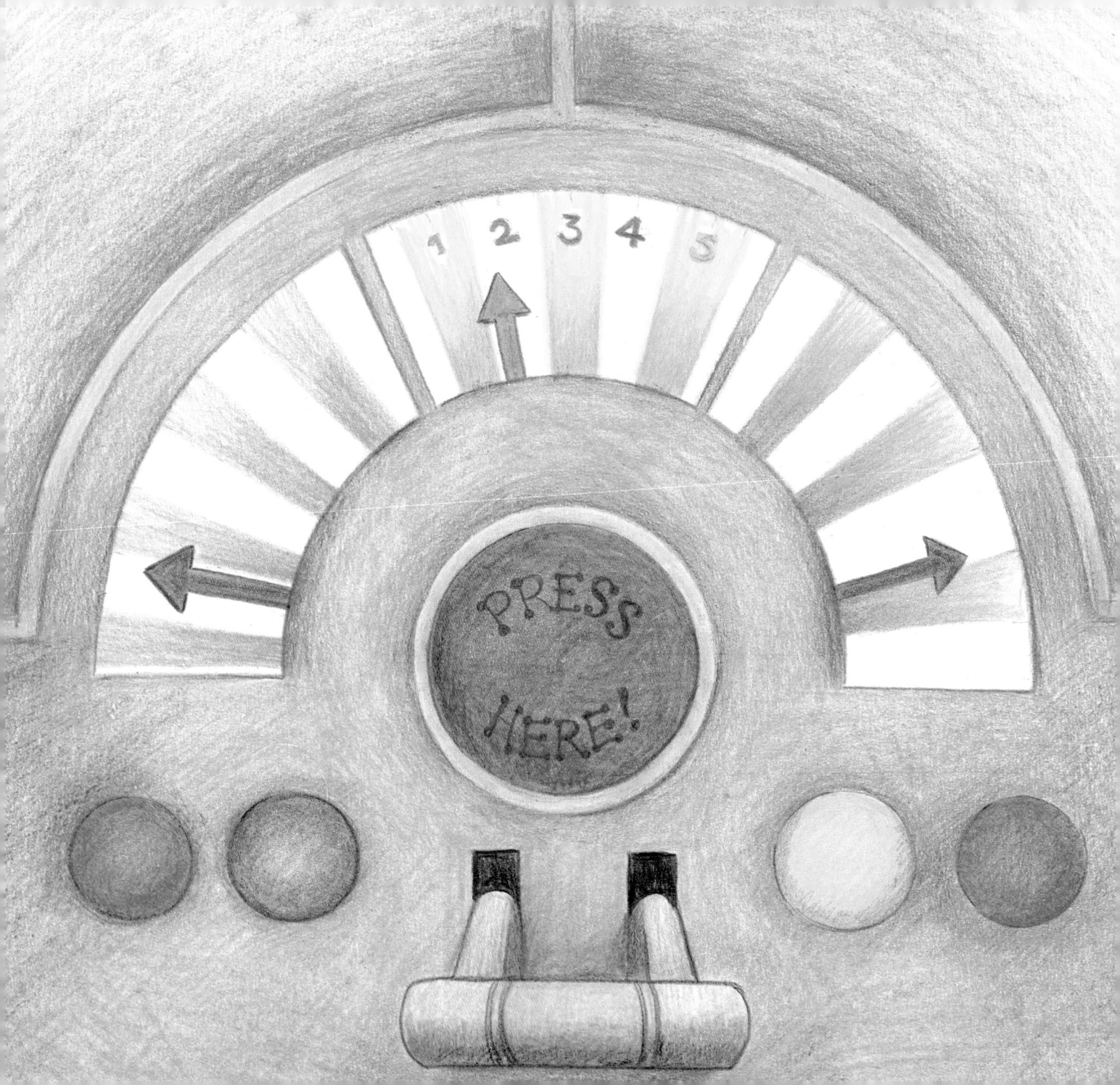

With a press of a magical squeaker on the control panel, they were off.

"That's amazing," Tiny said. "Yes," replied the bear," anything can happen with our magic squeaks."

Some time later the helicopter touched down in the Land of Squeaks.

He was quickly taken to his hotel room by a very grand bear called Mr. Bumble. "When you have unpacked you must come downstairs to the reception hall. There is a surprise waiting for you," he said.

Tiny unpacked as quickly as possible. He was in such a hurry to get downstairs that he slid down the banister.

Bump! He landed on the floor. "Oh dear, that will teach me not to be in such a hurry."

There were dozens of bears waiting for him to arrive. When he did, there was a loud cheer. I feel like a star, he thought to himself.

Furry Bear presented Tiny with a parcel. He tore off the paper, and inside was a beautiful red sweater. "How lovely!" he said as he pulled it over his head. Then he noticed the squeak. "What's this for?" he asked.

Furry Bear told Tiny it was a magical squeaker. All he had to do was shut his eyes and think hard about whatever he wanted to do.

Tiny closed his eyes tightly, pressed his tummy, and wished he could fly. In an instant he was zooming overhead. Everyone laughed.

For the next few days Tiny Tiger made a lot of new friends. He had fun pressing his squeaker to make himself invisible.

Can you find him? Press the page and see.

When the time came to say goodbye, Tiny pressed his magical squeaker and thought hard about being back in the woods. In no time at all he was in his living room.

Goodness, I wonder if this has all been a dream. Then he looked down and saw the red sweater. He knew that it had been real after all.

As he climbed into bed that night, he laid his magic sweater over the end of his bed.

He closed his eyes and started to dream about all the adventures he was going to have.

Tiny Tiger is going to have many more adventures with his magic sweater.

Just wait and see!